DUMB JOEY

pictures by Cheryl Pelavin

Rita Golden Gelman

HOLT, RINEHART AND WINSTON

New York   Chicago   San Francisco

Library of Congress Cataloging in Publication Data

Gelman, Rita Golden.
  Dumb Joey.
  SUMMARY: Always in the way when his brother and
friends try to play, Joey finally proves he can be useful.
  1. City and town life—Fiction. 2. Brothers and sisters—
Fiction. I. Pelavin, Cheryl, illus.
II. Title.
PZ7.G2837Du   [E]   72-76580
  ISBN 0-03-091959-2

A HOLT REINFORCED EDITION

Published simultaneously in Canada by
Holt, Rinehart and Winston of Canada, Limited.

ISBN: 0-03-091959-2
Library of Congress Catalog Card Number: 72-76580

Printed in the United States of America

Designed by Aileen Friedman

FIRST EDITION

For Steve, Mitch, and Jan

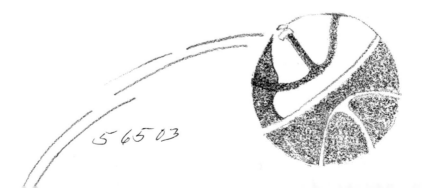

CONTENTS

CHAPTER ONE

Joey Gets Us in Trouble

My name is Punk.

His name is George.

His name is Crazylegs.

George, Crazylegs, and I

are real good friends.

We do everything together.

Every morning we meet on the street

and go to school together.

When school lets out,

we do things together.

3

There's just one other person.
My brother, Joey.

Joey is a pest.

I always have to take care of him.

If it weren't for Joey,

everything would be great.

But Joey is always in the way.

After school every day
we play stickball in the street.
One time when a car was coming,
I yelled, "Car!"
Crazylegs, George, and I
jumped out of the way fast.
But Dumb Joey picked up the bat
and just stood there
in the middle of the street.
The car almost hit Joey,
only it turned just in time
and hit a parked car instead.

What a mess!

A cop came and said he'd throw us in jail

if he caught us playing in the street again.

We stayed away for a couple of days,

but when we didn't see the cop around,

we started again.

But first, we had to do something

about Dumb Joey.

I don't like him much,

but I didn't want him to get hit by a car.

That's when I had my idea.

We got a rope

and tied Joey to a fire hydrant.

Joey wasn't too happy tied up like a dog.

But that was a lot better than

letting him be hit by a car.

Well, it was a great idea—
and it really worked.
Until that awful day.

George was at bat.
I was on first.
And Joey was tied up.
George is a pretty good player.
He's very strong.
I knew as soon as he hit the ball
that we were in trouble.
It smashed right through the window
of Gordon's grocery store.
Somebody yelled, "Run!"
And we did.

I was all the way down the alley

when I remembered

Joey.

Oh, no.

I sneaked a look.

There was Gordon and a cop.

They were just standing

next to Joey, waiting.

Dumb Joey.

Now what was I going to do?

I waited. So did Gordon.

So did the cop.

I waited some more.

So did Gordon and the cop.

I waited.

They waited.

It was starting to get dark.

I couldn't go home without Joey.

Finally, I just walked over
as though nothing had happened.
I started to untie Joey
when Gordon grabbed me.
"Your father's gonna pay for that, kid."
"For what, sir?
Did something happen?" I said.

I could feel my heart banging.

"Don't be a wise guy," said the cop.

"What's your name?

Where do you live?"

"Who me? I'm just picking up my brother.

What happened?"

That's when Joey said, "You know, Punk.

He means the window you guys broke

when you were playing ball."

I kicked Joey.

"That window cost two hundred bucks,"

said Gordon.

I reached in my pocket.

I had thirteen cents.

"Here," I said.

Gordon did a lot of screaming.

"I'll pay you when I grow up," I said.

"He can't pay," said the cop.

"But he better not come back here again.

Now, get out...."

Joey and I got out, fast.

CHAPTER TWO

We Discover Something

So that was the last time

we played stickball.

We tried a couple of times,

but Gordon was always there

with his mean face

saying he'd call the cop.

There were no other good stickball streets

in the neighborhood,

so we started going to Crazylegs' house.

No one was ever home there.

When we had nothing to do,

that's where we went.

We were just sitting in the bedroom one day

watching television

when we heard the crash.

We ran into the living room.

There was Joey, standing on the table.

A lamp was all broken on the floor.

"Joey!" we all screamed.
Crazylegs screamed the loudest
because he had to be there
when his mother came home.
We cleaned up the mess.
I left seven cents,
for Crazylegs' mother.
George had three cents and he left that.
No stickball.
No television.
No nothing.

So we started hanging around.
We hung around the candy store
until we got kicked out.
We hung around the street
just walking on walls and kicking cans.

We were just hanging around

the school one Monday

when I had an idea.

In back of the school there's a playground

with basketball hoops and everything.

We can only use it when the school is open

because the only way to get there

is through the school.

I figured that

if we could just get out there

after school let out,

we'd have the whole playground to ourselves.

So we sat down and worked out a plan.

George is the sneakiest.

So the next day

George hid out in the boys' bathroom

when school let out.

The rest of us just hung around outside.

George waited about half an hour

and then came to the side door.

"Okay," he said. "Come on in."

It felt real strange.

The building was empty.

We could hear our footsteps in the hall.

We walked to the playground door.

From inside the school,

all you have to do is push on the bar

and the door opens.

But once you're outside,

if you shut the door, it locks.

That was a problem.

We knew we had to put something in the door

to keep it open so we could get back in.

If the door slammed shut,

we'd be stuck in the playground

for the night.

I put one of my books in the door,

and we ran out to our playground.

It was great out there.

We ran all over the place.

We played with a basketball
George had swiped from the gym.
Even Joey wasn't in the way
because he played on the slide
and the monkey bars.
What a time we had.
When it was time to go,
we took the book out of the door
and went into the building.
It was dark.
We had to return the ball to the gym
and it was real scary in the dark.
We held hands in a line
as we walked up the stairs and down the hall.
When we got to the gym, the door was locked
so we left the ball in front of the door
and went back down the hall
and out the side door to the street.

We were all excited.

What a day!

What a great place to play.

Before we went home,

we made a secret pledge never to tell.

We made a circle and crossed our arms

and held hands. I said the pledge.

"If I ever tell, may I be shot down dead."

Then Crazylegs and George said the pledge.

"If we ever tell, may we be shot down dead."

Then we all went home. Boy, were we happy!

Every day that week

we hid outside until George opened the door.

And we always put the book

in the playground door,

so we never had any trouble getting out.

We stayed real late on Friday.

Me, George, and Crazylegs

were playing a lot of basketball.

"Watch this!" shouted George,

and he dribbled across the playground,

went in for a hook shot, and missed.

"That's easy," said Crazylegs

and he stole the ball from George,

dribbled in a circle,

went in for a hook shot,

and missed.

"Throw me the ball," I called.
I caught it and dribbled around my back
and through my legs.
Just as I was ready to show
how good I could dribble with my left hand,
I noticed Joey.
He was sitting against the wall,
reading a book.
I threw the ball down and ran to the door.
I knew it.
Joey had taken the book out.
We were locked in the playground.

CHAPTER THREE

Joey Uses His Head

We tried all the doors
just in case one was open.
They were all locked.
We didn't know what to do.
Crazylegs said, "Hey, if we had a rope,
we could throw it up to the roof
and climb up the wall.
Then we could slide down the other side."
George said, "I once heard of a man
who was made of rubber.
If I was made of rubber,
I could stretch up to the roof
and get us all out."
"If we were invisible,
we could walk right through the door,"
I said.

"I once heard that

if you held your finger

in front of your nose

and turned around twenty-five times

and then jumped,

you'd turn invisible."

"Do you think it works?" said Crazylegs.

"Let's try," said George.

And we all started to turn around.

I counted to fifteen and fell down.

George fell at twenty-one.

Crazylegs got to twenty-five and jumped.

But he fell before his jump landed.

We all lay there on the ground

and watched the world spin around.

We tried to play some more ball.

But we were all too scared

and couldn't make any baskets.

It started to get dark.

We knew our mothers were looking for us.

My mother would call George's mother

and she would call Crazylegs' mother

and she would call my mother

and they would all get mad together.

I could tell that

Crazylegs and George were scared.

I kept saying,

"Don't worry, we'll get out."

But I didn't know how.

I hugged Joey.

We started to feel hungry.

"We're having spaghetti for dinner tonight,"

I said.

"We're having hot dogs," said George.

Crazylegs said,

"I don't know what we're having,

but I wish you would shut up about food."

Joey kept saying, "I'm not scared."

It was real dark.

I said, "Aw, we'll get out okay."

Crazylegs said, "How?"

"We'll just get out, that's how."

"Suppose they never find us

and we starve to death?" said George.

"There's school on Monday," I said,

"and that's only three days from now.

People can't starve to death

in three days....

I don't think."

"See," said George,

"that means you really don't know."

"Well," I said,

"they'll find us before Monday, anyhow."

"Our mothers will call the cops,"

Crazylegs said, "and when they find us,

they'll put us in jail.

I don't want to go to jail."

"Me neither," said George.

"It's all *his* fault."

And he pointed to where Joey was....

only Joey wasn't there.

"Joey."

"Joey?"

"Hey, Joey," we all called.

No answer.

But there was no way out.

Where could he have gone?

"Joey!"

"Joey!"

I felt tears starting to come in my eyes.

"Joey…don't play games.

Where are you?" I called.

Only Joey wasn't there.

My heart was banging.

Tears started dripping down my face.

"But where could he go

if we're all locked up?"

asked George.

No one could figure it out.

Joey was still missing

when we heard a noise in the school.

Then a light went on.

We ran to the door and there was Joey

and the cop from Gordon's grocery store.

"Hi," said Joey.

I put my arms around him.

It was part hug and part squash.

"How did you get out?" I asked.

Joey took me by the hand

and walked around

to the far side of the playground.

There was the tiniest crack

between the end of the school

and the next building.

Joey turned sideways and went out.

He came back in.

"Let me try," I said.

I turned sideways.

My legs fit.

My body fit.

But my head was too big.

"Okay, you guys, let's go," said the cop.

And he walked us back to the open door.

"You guys better not do that again."

"Oh, no sir, we won't," I said.

"Never," said George.

"We'll never play in the playground again,"
said Crazylegs.

"I mean," said the cop, "you'd better not put
a book in the door.

That was pretty dumb.

The next time you go out there,

take this piece of rope

and tie it around the door handles like this.

Then you won't lock yourselves out again."

And when he finished talking,

he smiled a funny smile,

shook our hands, and left.

"Did you hear what I heard?" I said.

"Yea, wow," said George.

"I can't believe it," said Crazylegs.

"Okay, guys," said Joey.

"Let's go home, I'm hungry."

ABOUT THE AUTHOR

Rita Gelman was born and grew up in Bridgeport, Connecticut. After graduation from Brandeis University, she settled in the Greenwich Village area of New York City. Today she lives there with her husband, their two children, one dog, and seven puppies.

Of the city Ms. Gelman says, "Helping two children grow up here has made me aware of the incredible anti-child environment that exists. Kids can't play ball, walk on walls, write on sidewalks, or climb trees. They can't even ride their bikes in the neighborhood or make noise in their apartments. And they really *are* locked out of many playgrounds and empty lots. In their search for ways to express themselves and their energies, children have to sneak into forbidden and often dangerous territory. Somebody, somewhere, had better notice."

In 1968 when a teachers' strike locked New York City schools for more than two months, Ms. Gelman was one of a group of parents who sneaked into the local school at night in order to open the doors for the children. "While writing *Dumb Joey*," she says, "the experience of the dark hallways, the empty building, and the fear of being arrested—all came back to me."

ABOUT THE ARTIST

Cheryl Pelavin studied art at the Tyler School of Fine Arts, Pratt Institute, and Cornell University. This young artist's distinctive style has quickly established her as an illustrator and she has also written three picture books of her own.

A native of Brooklyn, New York, Ms. Pelavin now lives in Manhattan where she shares a studio with her cat, Michelangelo.

ABOUT THE BOOK

This book was set in Caslon No. 3 Linofilm. The artist pre-separated her art and used lithocrayon and gouache. The book was printed by offset.